Rabbi Rocketpower
And the
Half-Baked Matzah Mystery
A Particularly Peculiar
Passover

Why is this Matzah different from all other Matzah?

Written by
Rabbi Susan Abramson

Illustrated by
Ariel DiOrio

OAK LEAF SYSTEMS

MASSACHUSETTS   VIRGINIA

Rabbi Rocketpower
and the
Half-Baked Matzah Mystery -
A Particularly Peculiar Passover

by Rabbi Susan Abramson

Illustrations by Ariel DiOrio

~ ~ ~ ~ ~

First Printing

October 2009

~ ~ ~ ~ ~

Library of Congress Catalog Card Number: pending
ISBN: 978-0-9659546-6-2

Published by:
Oak Leaf Systems   Massachusetts   Virginia

~ ~ ~ ~ ~

A portion of the profits from this book
will be donated to charity.

www.rabbirocketpower.com
Printed on Unleavened Recycled Paper

In honor of

Carol Feltman

Fran Landry

Susanna Natti

whose generosity of time, talent, and
expertise has enabled

Rabbi Rocketpower to blast off

and continue on her mission.

ABOUT THE AUTHOR

Rabbi Susan Abramson is a graduate of Brandeis University and Hebrew Union College – Jewish Institute of Religion. She received her Doctor of Divinity degree from Hebrew Union College in 2006.

She has been the rabbi of Temple Shalom Emeth in Burlington, Massachusetts since 1984.

ABOUT THE ILLUSTRATOR

Ariel DiOrio is an illustration student at Massachusetts College of Art and Design. She loves to read picture books for children of all ages. She plans to pursue a career in art and hopes to use her artistic superpowers for *tikkun olam*, making the world a better place.

CONTENTS

A Half-Baked Passover History Mystery

A HALF-BAKED PASSOVER HISTORY MYSTERY
by Aaron
It was a really long time ago.... in Egypt.
This Sphinx!
Could you pass me that brick?
I hate my job.
The Israelites were slaves.
G-d sent a whole bunch of plagues so Pharaoh would let them go.
1
2
3
4
5
6
7
8
9
10

CHAPTER ONE

PURR'S FIRST PASSOVER?

Kaboom! A big box of crackers tumbled onto the kitchen floor, scattering crumbs in all directions.

"Oops," giggled Purr. She sat down in the middle of the kitchen table and wagged her tail.

"Oh Purr, I just finished sweeping," moaned Aaron, as he ran over with his broom and dustpan. "We have to clean the house and get rid of all the *hametz* before *Passover*."

"Hametz? Sounds like a disease. I hope I don't catch it," Purr screeched.

"It's not a disease. It's food that gets puffier when you cook it. You can't eat it on our Jewish holiday called Passover," Aaron explained.

"What? You have a holiday where you only eat flat food? That's the weirdest thing I ever heard," Purr replied, rolling her eyes.

"We eat flat bread called matzah to remember that our ancestors didn't have time for their bread to rise when they escaped from Egypt," Aaron continued, ignoring her.

"Wanna join us for our Passover *seder* tonight? You can hear the whole amazing story," Aaron suggested.

"Let's see. You're going to eat flat food, pass over cider, and tell a whole story?" Purr yawned. "I'd love to join you, Bub, but I think I have a play date with a dust ball."

"It's one of the best meals we have all year. And I said 'seder' not 'cider.'" Aaron chuckled. "'Seder' means 'order' in Hebrew. There's a special way we're supposed to tell the Passover story."

"Sounds exciting, Bub, but I think I hear a spider calling my name," she snickered. She stuck her tail in the air and pranced toward the living room.

Purr couldn't wait to see if her favorite spider, who had a web in a corner of the living room, had caught more bugs for her to play with. But the second she walked into the room – VROOOOM! A horrible loud noise nearly made her jump out of her skin.

"Yeeow!" she screamed as Rabbi Mensch began vacuuming.

"Hey, Bub, careful with that thing," Purr shouted. Rabbi Mensch pushed the vacuum toward the spider web in the back of the room.

"What? I can't hear you. I'm cleaning for Passover," yelled Rabbi Mensch, sending the spider scurrying to safety just in the nick of time.

"Passover, shmassover," Purr grumbled. "I need a snack."

She marched down the stairs to her basement hideout and stuck her head in her food dish.

"Not that same disgusting dry cat food again," she whined, scrunching up her nose. "Hey, maybe I'll try some of that Passover stuff in the kitchen. It couldn't be any worse than this dry rubbish."

CHAPTER TWO

THE MATZAH HAS A BALL

Purr snuck upstairs and tiptoed over to a shopping bag in the corner of the kitchen. She stuck her head inside to see if there was anything good to eat.

"The guy at the store gave me that bag of open matzah boxes for free. Isn't that great?" said Aaron excitedly. "One of the boxes was full of crumbs, so Mom said I could try making a matzah ball out of them."

"Sounds crunchy," thought Purr. She leaned a little further into the bag.

"Hey Mom, I thought matzah was dry," Aaron complained as his mother joined him in the kitchen.

He held up a big gooey glob. "These crumbs feel kind of slimy. I didn't even need to add water to make them into a ball," he added, making a face.

Purr was so hungry that she stuck her head completely inside one of the boxes. Just as she was about to take a bite out of a big sheet of matzah, it crumbled to the bottom of the box.

She tried to bite a second sheet, but it attached itself to the side of the box.

She tried to sink her teeth into a third piece, but it grabbed her nose and honked it like a horn.

"Ouch!" screamed Purr, losing her balance. She fell right into the shopping bag with her head stuffed into a matzah box.

"Help!" she yelled, running through the house. Inside the box, little pieces of matzah bounced on her nose as if it were a trampoline.

Aaron dropped the matzah ball on the kitchen counter and chased after Purr into the living room. She looked so funny that he couldn't help but giggle. But when his mother walked in and saw that Purr had left a trail of crumbs behind her, she wasn't very happy.

"Stop!" shouted Aaron. "Stand still and we'll get the box off of you."

"What? I can't hear you," Purr yelled. "And who turned out the lights?"

Rabbi Mensch finally managed to free her.

"It's about time," Purr huffed. "I'm outta here."

Purr ran down to her room in the basement and flicked on her Cat TV. She sat in front of it, munching her cat food and complaining under her breath.

Upstairs in the living room, Rabbi Mensch picked up the matzah box. "Aaron, does this smell a little like horseradish to you?" she asked, making a face.

"Maybe it's horseradish-flavored matzah," Aaron suggested. "I bet they invented it so you don't have to bother dipping the matzah into the *maror*, the bitter herbs, during the seder."

"That's an interesting idea," agreed Rabbi Mensch, not quite convinced. "I'll go get the vacuum."

Aaron ran back to the kitchen to finish his matzah ball. But it wasn't on the kitchen counter.

"That's weird," he murmured. He looked in the sink, on the floor, even in the refrigerator, but he couldn't find it anywhere.

Rabbi Mensch returned to the living room to vacuum up the crumbs. But when she looked at the floor, it was completely clean.

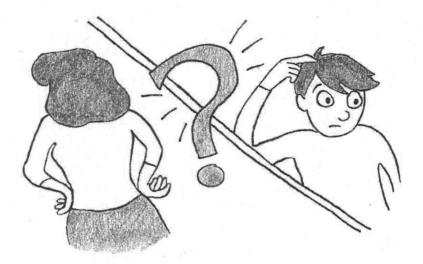

"Purr!" they both shouted.

"Did you take my matzah ball?" asked Aaron.

"Did you lick up all the matzah crumbs?" asked Rabbi Mensch.

"You matzah ball heads blame me for everything," Purr whined, as she appeared at the top of the basement stairs. "I wouldn't touch that matzah stuff if you paid me a million mice."

Aaron and his mother shrugged. They headed into the kitchen to begin setting the seder table.

He picked up the Passover bowls stacked on the kitchen table and found the matzah ball hidden behind it. He was absolutely sure he had left it on the kitchen counter. "How did my matzah ball get over here?" asked Aaron.

Purr grabbed her best friend Shmaltzy, a small, furry, yellow, chicken, catnip, squeaky toy, from behind the living room door. She curled up with Shmaltzy on the living room couch, ready to take a nap.

But as soon as she closed her eyes, she began to feel tickly little pinches on her fur.

Purr looked up, shocked at what she saw. There were the crumbs from the matzah box, marching from behind the seat cushion onto her back like an army of ants.

"Run for your life!" she screamed to Shmaltzy. Purr shook herself off and ran out of the room, forgetting that Shmaltzy couldn't run because she was a furry chicken squeaky toy.

Purr hid behind the door and peered around the corner. As she stared in amazement, the crumbs morphed into a matzah ball, bounced off Shmaltzy onto the floor, and rolled around the room.

"Are you guys ready to search for breadcrumbs?" Rabbi Mensch called out while she finished wiping off the kitchen table. "It's time to make a fire in the backyard to burn the hametz."

"Yay!" shouted Aaron. He opened the kitchen drawer whcre they kept the big white feather.

"This is my favorite part. I love to sweep up all the little crumbs with the feather and throw them in the fire. Wanna join us, Purr?"

"Sure, Bub. Let's start with the big fat crumb you missed in the living room," she teased.

"I just checked in there, but if you really want me to…" sighed Rabbi Mensch.

Purr sat back and laughed into her paw as Aaron and Rabbi Mensch walked back into the room. Just before they arrived, the matzah ball rolled behind the living room chair. When they started heading for the chair, it grew tiny little scrawny legs and tiptoed behind the couch. When they bent down to look behind the couch, it jumped into the living room plant and crumbled into little pieces on top of the dirt.

"This room looks perfectly clean," said Aaron. He and his mother took the bag of breadcrumbs they had already found, made a fire outside in their brick fireplace, and tossed in the bread.

"Purr, where are you?" yelled Aaron when the crumbs began to pop into red hot ashes. "I thought you wanted to see the bread burn. It's really cool."

"Sorry, Bub. I'm busy watching that crumb you missed." She giggled, peering into the living room. She was still too afraid of it to go in and rescue Shmaltzy. But she couldn't wait to see what that crazy matzah ball would do next.

CHAPTER THREE

SETTING THE SEDER TABLE

Aaron and his mother came back into the house, smelling like smoke from the fire.

"Everyone's going to be here soon and we've still got so much to do," groaned Rabbi Mensch as she looked at the clock. "Quick! Let's heat up the matzah ball soup. I have a special pot you can use for your matzah ball. Then we'll boil the eggs, take out the fruit and nut *haroset* we made this morning, finish setting the seder table, and get cleaned up."

"Can I put out the matzah from those other open boxes?" asked Aaron.

"Sure," said Rabbi Mensch. "I'll get the seder plate and the *haggadah* books I just bought. I can't wait to use them. They have a great new way to tell the Passover story."

"I'll jump on the table and lick all the plates to make sure they're clean," Purr offered. She continued spying on the matzah ball in the living room.

Aaron and his mother ignored that remark. They unfolded a fancy white tablecloth onto the dining room table and then carefully put out the special white Passover dishes with the gold rims.

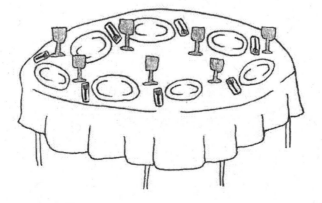

They put a *kiddush cup* at each setting, for the four cups of wine they would drink during the seder.

Aaron ran into the kitchen and grabbed a box of matzah out of the bag.

"No fair," he cried, looking inside. "There are only three pieces in this one."

"Well, that's all you need for now," his mother responded, lifting the *Elijah's cup* out of the china cabinet. "We can use them for the three *matzot* we hold up during the seder. When we break the middle matzah and hide it for the *afikoman*, you'll be able to find it more easily because of the smell."

"What? We're gonna hide a smelly awful con man?" yelled Purr from the living room doorway. "Maybe this cider thing is gonna be better than I thought."

"It's 'seder,' not 'cider.'" Aaron laughed. "And it's 'afikoman,' not 'awful con man.' 'Afikoman' is the Greek word for dessert. We break the middle matzah and put it in a special *afikoman bag* that a grownup hides during the seder. After we eat, the kids get to look for it and whoever finds it wins a prize."

"You mean if I find that awful guy I can get some catnip with the cider?" asked Purr.

"It's 'afikoman' and 'seder,'" Aaron and Rabbi Mensch said together, as they put the special foods on the seder plate.

There was maror, horseradish for the bitterness of slavery; *beitzah*, a hard-boiled egg representing new life; haroset, a fruit mixture that looks like the cement the *Israelites* used to build the *pyramids*; and *zaroa*, a roasted lamb bone to remind us of the sacrifices the Israelites made to thank G-d for keeping them safe.

"Now for the finishing touch," Aaron announced, running into the kitchen and returning with an orange. "I love the story about how someone said that women should be rabbis as much as an orange belongs on a

seder plate." He proudly placed the orange in the middle of the plate in honor of his mother.

Aaron put out bowls of salt water so everyone could dip their parsley to taste the tears the Israelite slaves shed in Egypt.

He put out a *Miriam's cup* in honor of Miriam who helped give the Israelites water in the desert.

Rabbi Mensch put a haggadah next to each person's plate. As Aaron lifted the three matzot out of the box, he couldn't figure out why they felt a little slimy. He hoped that Purr hadn't licked them.

Aaron decided the matzot were good enough, so he put them on a matzah plate, covered them with a *matzah cover,* and placed them gently on the table.

Then he took matzah from the other boxes and put a piece on each person's dish.

"Time to get dressed," declared Rabbi Mensch as she and Aaron rushed upstairs. They were excited about the seder. But as they changed into their fancy clothes, they had no idea just how exciting this seder would be.

CHAPTER FOUR

THE UNSUSPECTING SEDER
GUESTS

As soon as everyone was upstairs, Aaron's matzah ball jumped out of the pot, turned off the heat, then dived back in.

Purr left her post by the living room door to run into the bathroom and take a quick drink out of the toilet.

When she came back and peeked around the corner, she came face to face with a matzah cat.

"Eeeeek!" they both screamed.

As Purr ran for cover behind the door, the matzah

cat crunched its way across the hall and into the dining room. Purr grabbed Shmaltzy. They ran into the dining room just in time to see the matzah cat leap onto the table, crumble into a hundred tiny pieces, and spread out in all directions. Some of the crumbs slid into the haggadahs. Others plopped into the kiddush cups. Some attached themselves to the pieces of matzah on everyone's plates.

"This sadder is going to be happier than I thought," Purr exclaimed in amazement.

"It's 'seder,' not 'sadder'!" said Aaron, appearing next to her wearing his best gray pants and new white shirt. He was glad that Purr was suddenly looking forward to the seder. But something about her change of attitude made him a little suspicious.

Just then they heard a car door close. Aaron was excited that his friends, Kailee and Talia, and their parents, Martin and Aviva, would be joining them. He was particularly excited to see what Talia would do, since she was only one and a half years old. And he couldn't wait to taste Aviva's awesome *chocolate-covered matzah brittle.*

He opened the front door before they had a chance to ring the doorbell. Talia came bounding in, followed by four-year-old Kailee. Martin and Aviva carried in big plates of dessert.

"Kitty!" Talia shouted, stretching out her arms and running toward Purr.

"Give me a break," Purr groaned, running for cover under the dining room table.

After everyone was seated at the table and Talia was safely in her booster seat, Purr came out of hiding.

"Hey, Buster," Purr whispered to Aaron after jumping in his lap. "This saner is gonna be crazier than I thought."

"It's 'seder,' not 'saner,'" Aaron whispered back impatiently. "And why do you think it's going to be crazy?"

Before Purr could answer, Rabbi Mensch cleared her throat to begin.

CHAPTER FIVE

THE CRUMBIEST SEDER EVER

Rabbi Mensch began, "It's so great to have you all here to celebrate our ancestors' freedom from *slavery* in Egypt.

"I'm really thrilled about this new haggadah because it tells the story of the Israelites' journey from slavery to freedom so beautifully."

Everybody picked up their *haggadot*.

"Mom, my book is full of crumbs," Aaron complained, as matzah crumbs fell out of his book.

"Where did you get these from, a matzah factory?" Dad kidded, as crumbs fell out of his book too.

Everyone laughed as they shook the crumbs out of their books.

"Let's just turn to page one and sing the order of the seder," Rabbi Mensch suggested, shaking her head.

But when they opened their books to the first page, all they saw were the words

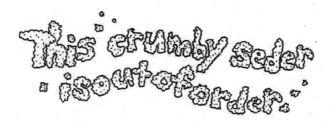

"What?" Dad laughed. "I know. You got these books from a joke shop. I thought the seder was supposed to be serious."

"Let's just turn to *Kadesh* on page two, to thank G-d for freeing the Jews from Egypt." Rabbi Mensch sighed. She stood up and read out loud, "Today we remember how poor Pharaoh was unfairly forced tolettheJewsleaveEgypt."

"Huh?" exclaimed the others, looking at Rabbi Mensch.

"How come some of the words are scrunched together?" asked Martin.

"I know this is a new way of telling the story, but don't you think it's being a little too nice to Pharaoh?" asked Aaron.

"Someone must have typed the words wrong," Rabbi Mensch grumbled.

Purr tried so hard to keep from laughing that she snorted.

Rabbi Mensch frowned at her and continued, "Aviva, you have the honor of lighting the holiday candles. The blessing is on page three."

Aviva stood up, lit the candles, and read, "We praise you, Pharaoh. You should be the king of the universe. Wewanttobeyourslaves."

"What?" everyone shouted.

"There must have been some problem at the printers," moaned Rabbi Mensch. "Let's just turn to page four to recite the *Kiddush*, the blessing over the first cup of wine. Martin, would you lead us, please?"

Everyone filled their cups with wine and stood up to recite the blessing.

Martin raised his cup and read, "We bless you, Pharaoh. You are thecrunchiestdudeever."

"How come I can't understand some of the words you're saying?" asked Kailee, getting frustrated. "What language is it supposed to be?"

"Is it my imagination or is this wine a little crunchy?" asked Dad, making a face after he took a sip from his kiddush cup.

"Mom, there's only one question on the page where there are supposed to be four," Aaron reported. "And it looks like it's all one really, really long word, 'Whydon'tyouforgetaboutthissederandgobacktoEgypt?' I can't figure out what it means."

Purr jumped off her chair and ran down to the basement so no one could hear her laugh.

"Look!" shouted Kailee, who was just learning how to read. "On this page there's a picture of four children. I remember that story. It's about how they all know Passover in different ways. But here there are four smiling children wearing matzah hats and waving on a pyramid. There's some long word over their heads that I can't figure out, 'comeondowntheweather'sfine.'"

"What kind of *ten plagues* are these?" asked Dad, turning to the middle of the book. "The plagues were supposed to be so bad that they made Pharaoh change his mind and let the Jews go free. But these are called The Top Ten Reasons WhyWeShouldMoveBackToEgypt.

"The first plague was supposed to be when the rivers turned to blood. But here it says the rivers are like yummystrawberrymilk. The second one was supposed to be frogs, not chocolatecoveredmatzahfrogs.

"The third was supposed to be people covered with lice, not peoplecoveredwithmatzahballs. The fourth was supposed to be wild beasts, not dancingkittensandpuppies. The fifth was supposed to be cattle disease, not cowsplayingcatchwithamatzahball…"

"Enough!" cried Rabbi Mensch. She turned to the last page. Instead of saying, "Next year in Jerusalem," it read, "Matzah matter with you people? This year youshouldallgobacktoEgyptandbePharaoh'sslaves!"

"I'm sorry. This is the worst haggadah I've ever seen," she apologized, shaking her head.

CHAPTER SIX

MATZAH MATTER WITH THIS SEDER?

Rabbi Mensch tried hard not to show the others how upset she was.

"It's a good thing I know the seder by heart. Let's continue with *Yahatz*, the ceremony for breaking the middle matzah."

She held up the plate with the three matzot and continued, "This is the bread our ancestors ate when they were treated badly in Egypt. Today we feel like slaves. Next year may we all be free."

Purr jumped into the air to try to get a better look at the plate.

"Givemeabreak," a high voice squealed from under the matzah cover.

"Purr, that's not nice," scolded Aaron. "The whole point of the seder is to remind us to be nice to people who need our help."

"Speaking of giving something a break," said Rabbi Mensch before Purr could talk back, "I will now break the middle matzah to show that our world is broken. I'm going to put that piece of matzah in the afikoman bag for the children to find after dinner."

As she stuck her hand between the two outer pieces of matzah to break the middle one, Purr threw Shmaltzy in the air so he could see what would happen.

"Ouch! You'recrackingmeup," chirped a high squeaky voice.

"Shmaltzy, was that you?" asked Aaron, giving Shmaltzy a really weird look as Purr caught him in her mouth.

Rabbi Mensch put the broken piece of matzah into a white felt bag with the word "afikoman" written on the front in gold glitter. Aaron had made it specially for the seder.

She held up the bag and explained, "I'm going to hide this when no one is looking. Whoever finds it after dinner will get a prize."

"Yay!" shouted Aaron and Kailee.

"Yay!" shouted Talia even though she didn't know why she was so excited.

"Ah-choo!" rumbled something inside the afikoman bag.

Purr laughed so hard that she rolled on her back, nearly squishing Shmaltzy.

"Please cover your nose when you sneeze, Purr," suggested Dad.

"You dodos blame me for everything. Come on Shmaltzy. We're outta here," Purr exclaimed. She grabbed Shmaltzy, stuck her tail in the air, and trotted into the kitchen. They hid behind the kitchen door to keep an eye on the afikoman bag.

"Time for the real Four Questions," Rabbi Mensch explained. "Why is this night different from all other nights? This year I can think of far more than four

reasons. I'll give you five minutes to see how many
you can remember. Ready, set, go!"

While everyone tried to think of the actual Four
Questions, Rabbi Mensch slipped out of the room with
the afikoman bag. She snuck through the kitchen,
through the family room, and out the porch door. Purr
followed right behind her, squeaking Shmaltzy all the
way.

"Can you please be quiet? You'll spoil all the fun,"
Rabbi Mensch whispered when she walked back in
from the porch without the bag.

"Who me?" asked Purr, innocently batting her eyes.
She dropped Shmaltzy next to the porch door so they
could both watch the afikoman bag.

After everyone managed to remember the real Four
questions, Rabbi Mensch helped them recall the real ten
plagues. They dipped their pinkies into their wine. They
put a drop on their plate when they said the name of

each plague to show they couldn't drink all their wine and be happy when other people were suffering.

They sang "*Dayaynu*," the song that says it would have been enough if G-d had just helped the Israelites get free, but G-d kept helping them.

"Waaah! Me want food," Talia cried, just as Rabbi Mensch was about to explain what was on the seder plate.

"I guess this seder has gone on a little longer than usual," said Rabbi Mensch. "Maybe we should get Talia something to eat while we prepare the appetizers."

"I'll give Talia some of my special matzah ball soup," Aaron offered.

CHAPTER SEVEN

THE MATZAH GOES BALLISTIC

Everyone but Talia gathered in the kitchen to peel the hard-boiled eggs and put gefilte fish and chopped liver on serving platters.

Aaron grabbed a bowl and a big spoon to get Talia her soup.

"Mom!" he yelled as he looked in the pot. "Didn't you turn on the stove? The soup looks cold."

"Waah!" cried Talia, banging her pudgy little hands on the table.

"It's okay if the soup isn't hot," said Aviva. "That way she won't burn her mouth."

Aaron carefully placed the matzah ball in the bowl. He didn't understand why it began bouncing around after he put it in so gently. But he didn't have time to think about it when Talia screamed, "Me want soup! Me want soup!"

"This matzah ball should fill you up for a while," he announced, proudly placing the bowl in front of her then racing back to the kitchen.

Talia dipped her spoon into the soup. But when she tried to pick up the matzah ball, it opened its eyes, stuck its tongue out at her, and swam away.

"Ook at matzah ball," Talia giggled.

"Glad you like it," Aaron said with a smile, returning with a plate of celery sticks filled with chopped liver.

"Keep an eye on that awful con man guy. I gotta see what happens next," Purr whispered to Shmaltzy. She snuck back into the dining room and jumped onto Aaron's chair.

As soon as Aaron joined everyone else in the kitchen, the matzah ball jumped out of the bowl and shook itself off on the table. It blew a matzah whistle and all the matzah on the table morphed together into a mini matzah mobile.

Talia and Purr couldn't believe what they saw. The matzah ball jumped into the driver's seat, revved up its tiny engine, and flew off the dining room table. It landed in the kitchen doorway and made a sharp left turn under the kitchen table before anyone could see it.

"Bye bye, matzah," Talia waved.

"Quiet, diaper head," whispered Purr. "You'll spoil everything."

"Did you drop your matzah ball, Talia?" asked Aaron, hurrying in to help her. He looked all over the floor but couldn't find it. When he looked on top of the table, he didn't see any matzah at all.

"Talia, did you eat everyone's matzah?" he asked in amazement. "How could you even reach them if you were strapped in your booster seat?"

"Ook at matzah," Talia yelled, pointing toward the kitchen.

"Mom, all the matzah's missing," yelled Aaron, trying to figure out what happened. But when he saw Purr excitedly wagging her tail under the kitchen table, he got suspicious. Just after the matzah mobile

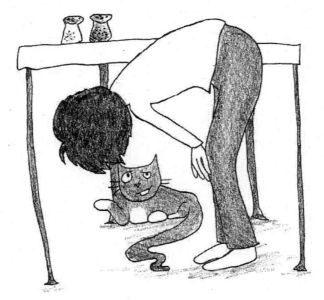

raced into the family room, Aaron stuck his head under the table.

"Purr, did you take the matzah?" he asked, although he thought that even Purr could not manage to be that sneaky.

"Sure, Bub. I made it into a car and drove it into the family room," she joked as she walked in that direction.

"That's ridiculous," Aaron responded. He looked all over the floor and scratched his head, trying to figure out what happened.

"Don't worry about it," said Mom, as she carried in a huge tray of *gefilte fish.* "Let's use the matzah from Israel I brought home this afternoon. It will remind us of the land of our ancestors when we say the blessings. I didn't like the way that other matzah smelled anyway."

Aaron gave everyone a new piece when they sat back down at the table. Rabbi Mensch explained what was on the seder plate and they recited the blessings over the matzah.

"The last thing we do before we eat is make a *Hillel sandwich.* We mix the bitter herbs and the sweet haroset to remember the bitterness of slavery and the sweetness of freedom," Rabbi Mensch explained. Everyone eagerly spooned maror and haroset onto their new matzah and made it into a sandwich.

As they enjoyed the appetizers, Aaron noticed that Purr was nowhere in sight.

"That's weird," he thought to himself. "I was sure she would be bugging us to give her some gefilte fish and chopped liver."

CHAPTER EIGHT

THE ROAMIN' AFIKOMAN

Everyone enjoyed their meal. After they had finished eating, Aaron, Kailee, and Talia played tag in the living room while the adults sat around the table talking.

"Calling all children," Rabbi Mensch announced. "Time to find the afikoman."

"Yay!" shouted Aaron and Kailee as they ran into the dining room.

"Yay!" shouted Talia, following after them, still not knowing why she was so excited.

"This year I hid the afikoman somewhere you probably wouldn't think to look. That's your only clue. Whoever finds it gets a special prize. Ready?"

"Me want Mommy!" Talia screamed, grabbing Aviva's arm.

"No fair. Then I want Daddy," Kailee whined, looking at Martin.

"Okay. We'll all go together," suggested Aviva.

"I don't need anyone to help me," Aaron announced. He was sure he knew where his mother had hidden the afikoman and he didn't want anyone tagging along.

"Ready, set, go!" shouted Rabbi Mensch.

Aaron ran into the living room and looked under each couch cushion. That's where his mother had hidden the afikoman for the last three years.

Kailee, Talia, Aviva, and Martin snooped around the kitchen and then headed into the family room.

Rabbi Mensch smiled as she heard them search behind bookcases and under the sofa. She turned on the water in the sink and began rinsing the dishes with Dad. The sound of the running water was so loud that they couldn't hear anything else.

"I looked all over the living room, the hall closet, and even upstairs under my bed," Aaron complained loudly as he reappeared in the kitchen. "I was sure you put the afikoman in one of those places."

"You've got a good memory," his mother remarked. "Those were all the places I hid it every year since you were old enough to look. Too bad our friends headed in the right direction." She grinned, looking toward the family room.

"Aw, man," Aaron moaned. "They must have found it by now. How come they didn't bring it back?"

"That's odd," his mother agreed, realizing that she hadn't heard any noise coming from that direction for a while.

Aaron rushed into the family room, hoping that somehow he still had a chance to find it first.

He didn't see any people, but he did see that the porch door was open.

"Aha," he whispered.

Aaron stepped onto the porch.

"Get back here, you rat," someone in the backyard screeched.

Aaron looked outside and couldn't believe his eyes. There was a big matzah mouse with the afikoman bag draped over its back like a saddle. It was zigzagging through the trees with Shmaltzy in its mouth, squeaking him as it ran.

Purr was chasing it, nipping at its matzah tail.

Talia was chasing Purr, shouting, "Here kitty!"

Kailee was chasing Talia, crying, "I found the afikoman first!"

Aviva ran after them holding two jackets, yelling,

"Put on your coats. It's chilly out here!"

Martin raced after Aviva, hollering, "We're going to miss dessert!"

Aaron looked up and his mouth dropped open. There in the clearing between the trees stood a huge pyramid made out of matzah. There was a big sign on one side that read, "AllIsraelitesWelcome." Under the sign was an open door.

The matzah mouse and all its followers were heading right for it.

CHAPTER NINE

PASSOVER PYRAMID SCHEME

Aaron ran into the kitchen as fast as he could. "Everyone's in the backyard chasing a matzah mouse with the afikoman bag on its back and they're heading toward a big matzah pyramid with an open door and a sign with one of those weird long words on it!" he shouted, out of breath.

"Huh?" asked Rabbi Mensch. She couldn't hear him over the running water.

"I'll get to the bottom of this," Dad shouted, throwing his dish towel on the counter.

He rushed upstairs and grabbed his trusty super laptop computer. He was back in a flash, searching the Internet for clues.

As Aaron tried to show his mother the pyramid through the kitchen window, Dad found an ancient cartoon that had recently been discovered floating in a bottle in the Red Sea.

The Original Half-Baked Matzah History Mystery
by The Original Aaron
The Israelites ran into the Red Sea.
Pit-ooey
Pharaoh was so angry that he spit into the matzah they left in the sand.
The spit was so full of anger that when the spit hit the sand the matzah morphed into the spitting image of Pharaoh and came to life.
It called itself the Pharaohcious Matzah Morphiac because its father was Pharaoh...
YAY Pharaoh
YAY Matzah
Its mother was matzah....
...and it realized that it could morph into anything it wanted.
YAY ME

"Huh?!?" Aaron and Mom exclaimed with puzzled looks.

"It says here that the ancient scroll was torn, so no one knows what happened next," Dad explained.

Suddenly they heard a loud, annoying voice coming from the basement.

"I can't stand that screechy Cat TV at a time like this!" Aaron moaned, rushing downstairs to turn it off.

"Cat-astrophc! Cat-astrophe!" a newscatter meowed on the screen as Aaron got closer. "Breaking Mews. The Pharaohcious Matzah Morphiac morphed into a shovel and dug underground all the way from Egypt to our neighborhood. It climbed out of a hole some people

had made to get a horseradish for their seder. Then it ran to the nearest supermarket and jumped into open boxes of matzah. Tell your humans to watch out. The Morphiac came to take them back to Egypt to be Pharaoh's slaves!"

"Oh, no!" yelled Aaron. He ran upstairs to tell his parents.

"So that's why the matzah smelled like horseradish," Rabbi Mensch realized.

"It must have morphed into crumbs and changed the words in our haggadahs," Dad realized.

"No wonder Purr was suddenly so interested in the seder," Aaron realized.

Before they could realize anything else, they heard a door crunch shut.

The Mensches looked out their kitchen window. The pyramid door was closed and the sign above it now read, "Thanksforvisiting. NextstopEgyptianslavery."

Putt, putt, putt. An engine started up. The pyramid lifted itself up on four big matzah ball wheels. Two matzah ball headlights appeared in front. It took off down the driveway and out into the street in a big puff of matzah dust.

"*Oy gevalt!*" Mom, Dad, and Aaron shouted at once.

CHAPTER TEN

RABBI ROCKETPOWER TO THE RESCUE

Before you could say "faster than a speeding matzah ball," Rabbi Mensch spun into the courageous Rabbi Rocketpower…able to wipe out evil wherever she finds it, able to make bad guys turn good with a flick of her mighty *yad*, able to make peace when there is war with her trusty *shofar*. She wore her blue outfit with the big white star in the front and her *tallis*-like cape on her back.

"Set the table for dessert. We'll all be back in a minute. Oy vay! Up, up and away!" she shouted to Aaron and Dad as she flew out the porch door.

She caught up with the speeding pyramid as it zoomed up the street. It was bouncing from side to side as if a lot of people were running back and forth inside it. She could hear shouting and complaining through the matzah walls. When it neared the top of a hill near the horseradish patch, a big matzah hatch opened in the back.

"Get lost, you paininthecrumb," the pyramid boomed. Purr came flying out on a matzah skateboard. The afikoman bag was covering her head. Shmaltzy was strapped to her back.

"I'm gonna get you, matzah breath," she screamed, rolling back down toward the Mensches' house.

Just as the hatch began to close, Rabbi Rocketpower zapped it with her mighty yad. With a snap and a crackle, it popped off.

Talia, Kailee, Aviva, and Martin jumped out, one after the other. They were all wearing striped prison uniforms made of egg and whole wheat matzah. They crunched down the hill after each other as fast as they could.

Talia ran after Purr, yelling, "Here, kitty kitty."

Kailee ran after Talia, shouting, "I found the afikoman first!"

Aviva ran after them with their jackets, yelling, "Get back here, it's cold!"

Martin ran after Aviva, shouting, "There better be some chocolate-covered matzah brittle left by the time we get back!"

As Rabbi Rocketpower changed their clothes back to normal with a blow of her mighty shofar, the pyramid's matzah ball wheels changed into rockets. It shot into the air, opened its trap door, and tried to pull her in.

"Comebacktoslavery," yelled the pyramid. But Rabbi Rocketpower was too quick for it. She ducked and darted out of its way.

She sounded her trusty shofar again and blew the pyramid into a rectangular matzah shape, with little arms and legs.

"Now that I've got your attention, I need to explain a few things," she said, holding it out in front of her. "I know how much you'd like to bring us back to Egypt. But do you know how terrible it is to be a slave?"

"It's fun," the matzah replied. "You get to buildprettypyramids and bakcinthesunallday."

"Did you know that Pharaoh made the Israelites work all day in the hot sun, even if they were sick or tired or really thirsty?" asked Rabbi Rocketpower. "And they couldn't do anything they wanted to do."

"But they helped Pharaoh build so many beautiful buildings. I thought they liked it," the Matzah Morphiac responded, a little confused.

"Their masters were very mean to them. They never got to play or have any fun. They were hungry and sad all the time," Rabbi Rocketpower continued.

The matzah looked surprised. "Really? I never knew aboutthatpart." It sighed.

"That's what our holiday of Passover is all about — for us to remember what it felt like to rush away from slavery into freedom," Rabbi Rocketpower explained.

"I guess that's why I was madeinsuchahurry," the Matzah Morphiac replied.

"Passover reminds us how easy it is for freedom to be taken away from us or anyone else. You helped us remember the story in a very... um...unique way," Rabbi Rocketpower responded.

The matzah shrugged. It couldn't decide whether it should be embarrassed, disappointed, or proud.

"Why don't you join us for the rest of the seder?" Rabbi Rocketpower offered. "We're about to welcome *Elijah the Prophet*, who gives us hope that the future will be better than the past. That should make us all feel a lot happier."

"Aslongas thatannoyingcat doesn't bother me," it said, shivering.

"Don't worry. We'll make sure that Purr doesn't know you're there," replied Rabbi Rocketpower, beginning to spin back into her usual self.

CHAPTER ELEVEN

ELIJAH NEVER COULD HAVE
PREDICTED THIS

Everyone sat around the dining room table enjoying scrumptious desserts. There were macaroons, brownies, chocolate chip *mandel bread*, fruit, and the all-important chocolate-covered matzah brittle. In the middle of the table was a large piece of matzah lying under the matzah cover.

"Purr is the winner of this year's afikoman contest!" Rabbi Mensch announced.

"The children all get a big chocolate lollipop for their efforts, but Purr gets the big prize."

"Yay!" squealed Talia as she grabbed her lollipop.

"Boo," Kailee pouted, crossing her arms.

"The only prize I want is to get back at that matzah maniac," screeched Purr from the living room, as she curled up with her furry yellow chicken. "No one messes with Shmaltzy and gets away with it."

Something groaned under the matzah cover.

"Okay, but I think you're going to like what I got you," shouted Rabbi Mensch, squeaking something behind her back.

Purr never could resist a squeaky toy. She trotted over to the dining room and looked around.

"Come and get it," Rabbi Mensch shouted, throwing a cloth matzah ball squeaky toy into the air.

Purr leaped and caught it in her mouth before it hit the ground. She ran under the table, yelling at it and then biting it as hard as she could.

The matzah cover shook.

"Is it windy in here?" asked Aviva, who couldn't understand why the matzah cover moved.

"That matzah brittle was so sweet that now I need to eat something plain," said Martin, licking his lips. "I think I'll just eat a piece of this matzah."

He reached over to grab the matzah. But it moved further under the cover.

"Huh?" he exclaimed, surprised.

"I want some too," said Kailee, who had just finished her lollipop. She reached under the cover and picked up the matzah. It jumped out of her hand and dove back under the cover.

"Mommy, the matzah flew out of my hand," she shouted in amazement.

Aaron and Dad looked at each other. They knew what was happening but couldn't say anything or else Purr would hear.

"Silly matzah," laughed Talia, whose face was covered with chocolate from the matzah brittle.

"What?" yelled Purr. Now she was suspicious. She jumped on a chair and stared at the matzah cover.

"Hey look, everybody. Do you see that this special cup is full of wine?" Rabbi Mensch asked, quickly changing the subject. She picked up Elijah's cup and showed it to the children.

"It's time to welcome Elijah the prophet. He comes to our seder every year to give us hope that the world will be a better place in the future and good things will happen to us if we try to help each other."

"Now open the front door and let him in," she told the children. "We'll know if he came if there's some wine missing when you come back."

"Come on, Purr," Aaron said, trying to distract her as she glared at the matzah cover.

"Don't bother me. Can't you see I'm busy?" she whispered.

Unfortunately, when Aaron opened the front door, the matzah stood up to look in the cup.

Just as the children squinted to try to see Elijah in the dark night, they heard a terrifying shriek coming from the dining room.

A matzah race car shot past them and sped out the door, screaming, "Get away, you pest!"

Purr followed close behind, shouting, "Get back here, you soggy old cracker!"

"Oh man, Elijah's never gonna come now. Purr and that matzah car scared him away," sighed Aaron, as Purr chased it around the front yard.

"Don't worry," Rabbi Mensch told the children. "Elijah's a very special prophet. A cat chasing a matzah car isn't going to keep him away."

She didn't say what she was really thinking, that if she were Elijah, she wouldn't want to come near a house where a screaming matzah car had just sped out the front door followed by a crazy cat.

After a minute, Rabbi Mensch called out, "Look what happened to the wine in Elijah's cup."

The children ran back to the table. Sure enough, half of the wine was gone!

"But I didn't see him," Aaron moaned.

"That's because he's invisible," his mother explained. "Now let's close the door so we can sing 'Eliyahu Hanavi – Elijah the Prophet.'"

Purr slipped back inside as Aaron closed the door. She sat down in the dining room doorway and let out a big, fat burp.

CHAPTER TWELVE

HAGGADAH GET OUTTA THIS PLACE

Rabbi Mensch frowned at Purr. "It's time to finish our seder. Let's open our haggadot and see what's in there now."

Everyone was relieved to find that the words were back to normal. Rabbi Mensch held up a special cup filled with water in honor of Moses' sister Miriam.

"Honk!"

They drank the third and fourth cups of wine.

"Honk!"

They ended by wishing for peace in Israel.

"Honk! Honk!"

"What's going on outside?" asked Aviva. She looked out the window but didn't see anything unusual.

"Our seder is over," continued Rabbi Mensch, trying to ignore the noise, "but we'll still eat matzah and food without *leaven* for the rest of the week. It will keep reminding us of how bad it is to be a slave and how easily freedom can be taken away. This year the Matzah Morphiac learned this lesson for the very first time."

"Honk! Honk! Honk!"

"Is there a car out there? I don't see anything," said Martin, peering out the window.

"Ugh," Purr moaned, as something pounded inside her tummy.

"Purr, did you eat something you shouldn't have?" asked Rabbi Mensch suspiciously.

"Honk! Honk! Honk! HONK!"

Aaron ran to open the front door to see what all the commotion was about.

"Blehhhh," Purr burped loudly.

"Get me out of here!" shouted a high voice. A matzquito buzzed out of Purr's mouth. It flew out the front door and jumped into the driver's seat of the mini matzah car that was waiting impatiently in the front yard.

"At least there are no annoyingcatsinthedesert," yelled the car as it sped toward the horseradish patch in the distance.

"I'm outta here," announced Purr, acting like nothing strange had happened. She stuck her tail in the air and headed for the basement.

The Mensch family and their friends looked at each other and shrugged.

Another holiday. Another adventure.

Checklist For A Purrfect Seder

What To Have On The Seder Table

Elijah's cup

Miriam's cup

Matzah plate with three *matzot*

Matzah cover

Afikoman bag

Bowls of salt water

Seder plate, including:

    1. Maror – horseradish
    2. Zaroa – shank bone
    3. Beitzah – roasted egg
    4. Karpas – green spring vegetable (parsley or celery)
    5. Haroset – fruit mixture (see recipes)
    6. Hazeret (not on all seder plates) – lettuce
    7. Orange in the middle (optional)

What Each Person Will Need

Haggadah

Kiddush cup

Parsley

Haroset

Maror

Matzah

Small pillow for back of chair (optional)

Hardboiled egg (optional)

All Set With Haroset?

Rabbi Rocketpower's Tutti Fruitti Haroset

Only make this recipe if there is an adult there to help.

Ingredients	Equipment
8 oz. sliced almonds	blender
16 oz. dried figs	large bowl
16 oz. dried dates	spoon
16 oz. dried apricots	
¼ - ½ cup Kosher for Passover wine or grape juice	

---

1. Combine small amounts of almonds, figs, dates and apricots in blender or food processor. (Don't worry about exact amounts. It will come out great no matter how much of each ingredient you put in.)
2. Put on "chop" setting (about 30 seconds).
3. Put on "blend" setting (about 30 seconds).
4. Carefully empty into bowl with spoon or spatula.
5. Repeat.
6. Add small amount of wine or grape juice.
7. Press down with spoon until it has a pasty texture.

Feeds 15. Make enough for the whole week!

Jamie's Hand-Me-Down Haroset

Only make this recipe if there is an adult there to help.

Ingredients	Equipment
4 large apples	cutting board
2 cups chopped walnuts	knife
2 T sugar	large bowl
4 T cinnamon	peeler
2 T grated lemon rind	grater
6 T sweet red wine	food processor

1, Peel, core and cut apples into chunks.

2. Chop apples coarsely in a food processor and place in a mixing bowl.

3. Add nuts, sugar, cinnamon and lemon rind.

3. Add wine in small amounts. Stir and taste.

5. Adjust ingredients as desired.

6. Refrigerate until serving.

Makes 6 cups.

Matzah Masterpiece

Aviva's Chocolate-Covered Matzah Brittle

Only make this recipe if there is an adult there to help.

Ingredients	Equipment
Plain unsalted matzah	large cookie sheet
1 cup brown sugar	parchment paper
2 sticks butter or margarine	medium pot
1 cup chocolate chips	large spoon
Crushed walnuts (optional)	knife

---

1. Pre-heat oven to 350 degrees.
2. Line cookie sheets with parchment paper or tin foil.
3. Cover sheet completely with matzah.
4. Heat brown sugar and butter in pot until it boils.
5. Pour over matzah.
6. Bake for 5-10 minutes until topping begins to bubble.
7. Remove from oven.
8. Sprinkle chocolate chips over matzah and smear with knife. If chocolate doesn't melt, bake for 5 minutes.
9. Sprinkle nuts if desired.
10. Refrigerate until it hardens.
11. Break into large pieces.
Makes enough for 5 people.

GLOSSARY

Afikoman – Greek word for "dessert." Near the beginning of the seder, a broken half of the "middle matzah" is put into a bag and hidden by an adult. After the meal, the child who finds it is supposed to get a special prize. At our house all the kids who look for it get a prize. The afikoman reminds us that the Israelites often had nothing more to eat than a broken piece of bread when they were slaves in Egypt.

Afikoman Bag – A special bag to put the afikoman matzah in so it doesn't get crumbs all over the house or leave a crumby trail that will make it too easy to find. Who wants crumbs in their drawers or on their floors or behind their doors? Try making one. It's fun!

Beitzah – Hebrew for "egg." A roasted egg placed on the seder plate as a symbol of mourning or sadness about what happened to the Israelites. It reminds us of new life and the circle of life. It is roasted to help us remember that the Israelites made a special sacrifice at the Temple in Jerusalem when it existed thousands of years ago. Don't roast it for too long. Rabbi Rocketpower did this once and it exploded all over her toaster oven!

Chocolate-Covered Matzah Brittle –
Delicious! See recipe page. Warning: this is not a diet food. Run around the block before and after eating.

Dayaynu –
Hebrew for "it would have been enough for us." It is the name of a song we sing during the seder that reminds us of the many miracles G-d performed for us, from letting the Israelites leave Egypt to giving us the Torah to observing the Sabbath. What miracles can you think of? We'd go on, but, dayaynu, it's enough already.

Elijah the Prophet –
One of the most important prophets in the Bible. A prophet is someone who spoke with G-d in ancient times and helped guide the Israelites to follow G-d's laws. According to the Bible, Elijah didn't die but went up to heaven in a chariot of fire. We believe that when he comes, it's a sign that good things will happen in the future.

Gefilte Fish –
Gefilte is the Yiddish word for "stuffed." Oval shaped cakes or balls made out of different types of white fish, plus a little matzah meal, a little egg, a little broth. Usually comes packed in jelly. Some people think the jelly part is delicious. Others think it is disgusting. Usually served as an appetizer at most Jewish holiday meals. Try it. You'll like it (maybe not the jelly part).

Haggadah (plural **haggadot**) – Hebrew for "telling." The name of the book which contains the service we have at the Passover meal, telling the story of the Israelites journey from slavery to freedom. We're supposed to add our own ideas to the story. Anything you'd like to say?

Hametz – Name of the foods which are not allowed to be eaten during Passover because they are leavened (that means they rise). This helps us remember how our ancestors rushed to leave Egypt. Foods made out of these five grains are hametz because they expand in water: wheat, barley, rye, oats, and spelt. Anything made with rice, corn, lentils, and beans are not eaten cither, except by Jews from some Middle Eastern backgrounds (we know it's really confusing!). Meat, fresh fruit and other vegetables are OK. The simplest thing to do on Passover is only eat fresh foods or non-fresh foods which say "Kosher for Passover" on the label.

You are supposed to get rid of your hametz before Passover begins. Here are some suggestions of what to do with it:

1. Bring it to a food pantry to help feed people who can't afford food.
2. Eat it all.
3. Sell it to a neighbor (then buy it back after Passover is over).

4. Store it away someplace where you won't be tempted to eat it.
5. Ask a grownup to burn the remaining crumbs you find around the house.

We recommend that you go with #1.

Haroset – From the Hebrew word "clay." Lumpy, fruity, pasty mixture which is supposed to remind us of the cement the Israelite slaves used when they were building pyramids in Egypt. See the recipes on the following pages.

Hillel Sandwich – Also called "korech" (sandwich in Hebrew). You put a little maror and a little haroset between two pieces of matzah. Why? One reason is to remember that there are always two sides to life, the sweet and the bitter, the happy and the sad, freedom and slavery. We are happy that we were freed, but we must remember that there are other people who need help. Rabbi Hillel was the very first one to make this sandwich in the 1st century B.C.E. so it was named after him.

Israelites – The name of the Jewish people beginning from when they lived in Egypt. They were given this name in honor of their ancestor Jacob, who was given the name Israel after he struggled with an angel in the desert.

Kadesh – From the Hebrew "to make holy." The first part of the seder after the candles are lit. This is when you drink the first cup of wine (if you're a kid it might be grape juice).

Kiddush – The Hebrew word "to make holy." The name of the blessing over the wine. We say the Kiddush four times during a seder. Do you know why?

Kiddush Cup – The special cup filled with wine or grape juice that you hold up when you say the Kiddush.

Leaven – Ingredients that make food rise or get bigger, like yeast.

Oy Gevalt – Oy Vay.

Oy Vay – Oy Gevalt.

Mandel Bread – Actually "mandelbrot." It literally means "almond bread." A hard biscuit type cookie you can eat on Passover. Really good with chocolate chips (at least that's how Rabbi Rocketpower likes them).

Maror – From the Hebrew word "mar" which means "bitter." The name of the bitter herbs you eat at the seder. It is often made out of horseradish. Once someone gave Rabbi Rocketpower a real horseradish root which cleared out her sinuses after the first bite. Watch out. This stuff is powerful.

Matzah (plural **matzot**) – The flat bread the Israelites took out of their ovens before it had a chance to rise when they were leaving Egypt. We suggest that you eat a lot of fruit and vegetables along with the matzah or else you will really suffer after a full week of Passover!

Matzah Cover – Special cloth you place over the matzah at the seder. You can make one yourself which will make the seder extra special.

Matzah Kitty – Don't ask.

Miriam's Cup – A cup honoring Miriam, sister of Moses, leader of the Israelite women. There's a legend that she had a magical well which followed her through the desert so the Israelites would have enough to drink. To honor her, everyone pours a little of their water into her cup.

Passover – Name of the holiday celebrating the Israelites' freedom from Egyptian slavery. Its name comes from the story of the 10th plague, when the angel of death passed over the Israelites' homes so they wouldn't be hurt.

Pharaoh – The ruler of Egypt. He was like a king. The name of this Pharaoh was Ramses II. Not a nice guy AT ALL. He made the Israelites slaves and stubbornly wouldn't let them leave.

Pyramids – Buildings with a square base at the bottom. The four sides slope up into a point at the top. In ancient Egypt they were made out of bricks and cement. Pharaoh forced the Israelites to build them.

Seder – Hebrew for "order." The name of the service Jews have on the first and often the second night of Passover. It is given this name because there is a special order that the service is supposed to follow.

Shofar – Ram's horn that Jews blow to announce the Jewish New Year (Rosh Hashanah) and the end of the Day of Atonement (Yom Kippur). Cooler than a siren! Try it sometime. Bet you can't make a sound come out of it.

Slavery – When you're held captive by other people and have to do what they say all the time. You don't have any choice in the matter. You can never do anything you want to do and you feel tired and sad. If you ever hear of anyone who is a slave you should try to help them. It's the Jewish thing to do.

Tallis – The prayer shawl Jews wear when they lead a worship service or when they pray during the day. It makes you feel special when you wear one, like you're being wrapped in a prayer or being hugged by G-d. Only adults are supposed to wear them, but that doesn't mean you can't try one on.

Ten Plagues – Moses and his brother Aaron asked Pharaoh ten times to let the Israelite people go. Each time Pharaoh said no. G-d punished Pharaoh by sending a really bad disease or really bad weather or some other really bad problem to the Egyptians.

Yad – Hebrew for "hand." You can't touch the holy Torah scroll with your fingers out of respect for its holiness. This is the name of the pointer you use so you won't lose your place.

Yahatz – The section of the seder when you break the middle of the three matzot on the matzah plate. The larger piece of the broken matzah is hidden as the afikoman.

Zaroa – The Hebrew word for "bone." It is the name of the roasted lamb bone on a seder plate. Some people use a chicken neck or a chicken wing. It reminds us of the lamb that was sacrificed by the Israelites to thank G-d for saving them from Egypt. It is not supposed to be eaten.

ACKNOWLEDGMENTS

This book would never have seen the light of day without the dedication, enthusiasm, and creativity of the Rabbi Rocketpower crew.

Ariel DiOrio, our illustrator, continues to bring her unique talent and keen eye to highlight the story. Her sense of humor shines through the expressions and perspective she uses to embellish the text and enrich the experience of the reader.

Neither of us could have completed this task without the oversight, enthusiasm, and wonderful spirit of Susanna Natti, our Art Director. She generously gave us the gift of her wisdom and expertise every step of the way.

Fran Landry spent innumerable hours making sure every jot and tittle of this book was as grammatically accurate as possible. This was after she spent innumerable hours challenging me to develop the plot and the characters, and debating the humor of words, phrases, and situations. There were many late nights on the phone when we laughed ourselves silly.

Neither this book nor this series would exist without the kindness, support, and generosity of Carol Feltman, publisher, friend, and Rabbi Rocketpower fan. She patiently taught me the ropes and helped produce the book itself. Thanks to Amanda and Rebecca Feltman for their suggestions and advice.

Thank you to Lisa DiOrio for maintaining and updating our website, www.rabbirocketpower.com, with creativity and expertise. I appreciate all the efforts of Joan Perlman, our marketing guru, who has worked tirelessly to promote the Rabbi Rocketpower series.

Thank you to Temple Shalom Emeth's 2008-2009 Fourth Grade Religious School class and to Carol Fanger Bell and the students at the South Area Solomon Schecter Day School for their very helpful comments.

Finally, thank you to my son Aaron, without whom the idea for this book and this series would never have come to be. It was in 2001, when he was in the first grade at the Rashi School in Newton, MA, that we developed these stories as a fun way to experience the Jewish holidays together.

Rabbi Susan Abramson, D.D.

August 2009

The reviews are in:

Rabbi Rocketpower's <u>Who Hogged The Hallah?</u> and
<u>The Mystery of the Missing Menorahs</u> are a blast!

It was hilarious. I loved it and I hope you will too.
Ethan, age 11

*This book is funny and fun for young or older
aged kids.*   Alex, age 10

*My daughter requested an immediate second
reading. How amazingly creative to have a
fun, suspenseful book with no bad elements.*
Marjorie (mother of Sydney, age 5)

*It teaches about Hanukkah while reading
the funny story. You should read this book.*
Amanda, age 9

*When I was 7 years old, I read this story
and I could even understand the big words
in it. If you want to know more about the
book, buy a copy!*   Rebecca, age 8

www.rabbirocketpower.com

"One Mitzvah Leads To Another"
Pirkei Avot Chapter 4, Mishnah 2

Watch for these upcoming Rabbi Rocketpower adventures:

A Tutti-Frutti Tale for Tu Bishvat

A Purr-fectly Preposterous Purim

Blintzes Rule/Cats Drool – A Cheesy Tale for Shavuot